Florence

was no ordinary

Fairy

Neil Griffiths

Illustrated by **Doug Nash**

Florence was no ordinary fairy.
For a start, she hated living at the
bottom of the garden!

(Well, wouldn't you?)

For Emma, a lovely friend and
a wonderful storyteller herself.

Red Robin Books is an imprint of Corner To Learn Limited

Published by
Corner To Learn Limited
Willow Cottage • 26 Purton Stoke
Swindon • Wiltshire SN5 4JF • UK
www.redrobinbooks.com

ISBN 978-1-905434-03-9

Text © Neil Griffiths 2007
Illustrations © Doug Nash 2007
First hardback edition published in the UK 2007
First paperback edition published in the UK 2007

Design by
David Rose

Printed by
Tien Wah Press Pte. Ltd., Singapore

It was damp and dark. What's more, bees often chased her, frogs leapt out of nowhere, and spiders sprang from dark corners to frighten her. So Florence now shared a toadstool with a pixie friend of hers in a neighbouring wood!

But that's not all that made her unusual, as Florence hated doing almost anything fairy-like …

… to begin with, she never told fairy stories as most fairies do, as she could never seem to remember them …

... she wouldn't leave 50 pence under any child's pillow who had lost a tooth, as teeth always made her feel completely queasy ...

… she hadn't ever appeared in a pantomime as a Godmother, or turned a pumpkin into a stagecoach, as she suffered from stage fright …

… she also avoided carrying wands, as they usually got caught up in her hair …

... neither did she scatter fairy dust, as she was allergic to the ghostly stuff and sneezed all day ...

… and of course she positively refused to sit at the top of the Christmas tree! It was most uncomfortable, she was scared of heights, and pine needles would get stuck in her pants for months!

(*So, would you?*)

In fact, Florence did very little at all, but she did have one fairy weakness – FAIRY CAKES! She adored them! (*Don't you?*)

Plain, chocolate chip, iced, currant, cherry-topped – quite frankly, any kind!

But her favourite was chocolate, with chocolate icing and chocolate hundreds and thousands on the top.

When she wasn't eating them, she was making them, and that didn't take long, as it was the one time her wand did get put to use. Two waves and an instant plateful appeared, and Florence was in fairy cake heaven!

There was, however, one problem!

VROOM!
VROOM!

Florence was putting on weight, lots of it. Things had got so bad one day that, to her horror, she found she was unable to fly.

She had a perfectly good set of wings, but they simply weren't strong enough to lift her, not even an inch off the floor.

News of this reached the Queen of the fairies, and Florence was summoned to the Fairy Palace!

"Florence, this simply won't do!" said the Queen. "No fairy of mine is going to be flightless. Why, you will ruin the reputation of the fairy kingdom."

"I'm sorry, your Majesty, but it's the fairy cakes!" whimpered Florence.

"I don't want to hear," grumbled the Queen. "I'm sending you to a fairy fitness farm, and I expect results!"

Florence tried to protest, but the Queen's mind was made up.

She was kept to a strict diet of carrot and cabbage soup, lettuce of every kind imaginable, and bowls and bowls of fruit salad. She even attended daily aerobic and yoga lessons! Finally, Florence was passed fairy fit and ready to nervously take her first flight.

Bravely she revved up her wings, then leapt into the air!

It was as if she had never been grounded. In fact, she felt like a new fairy!

She hovered,
swooped, soared and
even managed a
loop the loop!
(*Quite impressive,
don't you think?*)

Suddenly, feeling amazingly light winged, she decided to get her own back on the bees, frogs and spiders at the bottom of the garden and took her friend the pixie on a high-speed flight to remember!

(*Glad it wasn't me!*)

Florence was soon bursting with
newly-found confidence!

She came first in a fairy fun flight, appeared alongside Egbert the Elf as the 'Sugar Plum Fairy' in the Nutcracker ballet, and was crowned Fairy Slimmer of the Year!

However, as a now famous fairy, Florence hadn't changed much. She still lived happily in her woodland toadstool and firmly refused to do fairy-like things. But of course one thing had changed, she no longer ate fairy cakes.

Florence

rence
tage

Well, that's what
she tells us ...

... but I'm not sure
I believe her!
(*Do you?*)